I CARRIED THE CROSS

A STORY ABOUT SIMON OF CYRENE

I Carried The Cross
A Story About Simon Of Cyrene
By Lyle Wilkins

ISBN: 979-8-9917173-7-3

Prepared for Publication By

MAKING YOUR BOOK A REALITY
Fairmont, WV | 843-929-8768 | info@BandBpublishingLLC.com

To Contact the Author
Lyle Wilkins
lwdw77@yahoo.com

CONTENTS

Disclaimer

SIMON THE CYRENE

The story you are about to read is a fictional reimagining of Simon the Cyrene, who the Bible says helped carry the cross of Christ.

The Bible does not give us any additional information about Simon and this book is not intended to be a literal interpretation of the Bible and should not be considered a theological text.

Matthew 27:32 NIV

As they were going out, they met a man from Cyrene, named Simon, and they forced him to carry the cross.

Mark 15:21 NIV

A certain man from Cyrene, Simon, the father of Alexander and Rufus, was passing by on his way in from the country, and they forced him to carry the cross.

Luke 23:26 NIV

As the soldiers led him away, they seized Simon from Cyrene, who was on his way in from the country, and put the cross on him and made him carry it behind Jesus.

Chapter 1

THE INTRODUCTION

I will never forget that week of Passover in Jerusalem. What started out as a remembrance of how God delivered His people from slavery to the Egyptians turned into the beginning of a deliverance for all mankind from the power of sin. With Passover, it all began with the blood of a lamb spread across the doorposts, saving us from the death spread over Egypt. With salvation for all mankind, it began with the blood of ONE MAN poured out on a cross that washed away the sins of the world.

But how is this possible?

Today, as you lend me your ear and your heart, I want to share my story. I want to share the interaction that I had with this ONE MAN that changed my life forever. And this is a promise I can make to you, if you really hear, I mean really hear what I am about to say, I guarantee it will change your life as well.

Chapter 2

THE FIRST PASSOVER

It all started when the men of Cyrene took the annual trip to Jerusalem to celebrate Passover. I always found it so exciting because it was like traveling back in time. What do I mean by that? Well, let me just say that I never sat on the back of the camel asking, *"Are we there yet? Are we there yet? Are we there yet?"* I say this because my heart was so engaged with the stories we would hear from the older men in our group as they recalled the history of the Jewish people, and all that God had done for them.

It is kind of comical now that I think about it, because it would always start the same way. Benjamin, the oldest and wisest of our group, would say something like, *"Have I ever told you about how it all started?"* Once we heard that, many of us would smile at each other knowing we had heard this story every single year we traveled together, but it was an exhilarating story, a fascinating story, an inspiring story, and a true story I might add, that we never tired of hearing.

Benjamin would continue sharing how it all began with a guy named Abram and how God changed his name to Abraham, promising that He would make a nation of many people out of his family line. Without hardly taking a breath, he would continue, sharing the stories of Issac, Abraham's son, and Jacob, his grandson.

Then when he finally had stopped talking to breathe, Isaiah, one of the other elders in our group, would pick where he ended, or I should say he interrupted, because he was so excited to share the next part.

He would begin where Jacob's son, Joseph, went from being sold into slavery by his own brothers, to being raised to second in command in all of Egypt because he saved the known world from starving to death during a seven-year famine. Then he would share how Joseph also saved his entire family, even the same brothers that did him evil so many years before, which I must admit, if my brothers did that to me, forgiving them would be a hard thing to do. But even with the great things he accomplished, Joseph's fame would not last forever. After time had passed, a new king of Egypt came to power who did not know about him and all he had done.

Isaiah, while telling this story to our group, would recall the account that Moses wrote in the book of Exodus about this new king and what he said about the Israelites...

> *"Look, the people of the children of Israel are more and mightier than we; come, let us deal shrewdly with them, lest they multiply, and it happen, in the event of war, that they also join our enemies and fight against us, and so go up out of the land." (Exodus 1:9-10 NKJV)*

Then Benjamin, after having a long enough break from storytelling, jumped right back on, saying, *"So, do you know how that new king dealt with us? He put taskmasters to rule our lives and oppress us with forced labor. In our slavery, we built the cities of Pithom, Ramses, and other cities for the Pharaohs of Egypt. Then, when it seemed it could not get any worse, Pharaoh then ordered the midwives to kill every male child born to the Hebrews."*

During this part of the story, I would always seem to stop and begin to reflect on how people could be so cruel. You could feel the tension among the group grow and my heart would break from what the Jewish people had gone through. But usually about this time, Abigail, one of the elderly widows in our group, who was such a precious and kind person, would ever so softly change the whole mood of the story by saying, *"but don't forget, even in the middle of this atrocity God never forgot us. In His great mercy, God hid the son of a Levite woman when his mother placed him in a basket and set it afloat down the Nile River. Then, through God's divine hand of providence, Pharaoh's daughter found the basket, named the boy Moses, and raised him in the house of Pharaoh."*

"It was true," I thought to myself, God had divinely orchestrated His people's deliverance from their oppressors.

Then Isaiah, with a new boldness, picked the story back up, sharing, *"then after many years had passed, and Moses was grown, he went out one day and saw an Egyptian beating a Hebrew. Being caught up in the moment, he could no longer take the sight of his people being oppressed and he killed the Egyptian. But then, out of fear of what Pharaoh would do to him, he ran for his life and spent the next forty years in the desert."*

Then Benjamin would jump back in, *"That is, of course, until God told him to go back to Egypt and lead his people out of bondage, and into the Promised Land."*

He swiftly continued, so Isaiah could not take the story back over, *"but this would not be a simple task. When Moses told Pharaoh to let God's people go, Pharaoh said NO! God then brought nine plagues upon Egypt, boils, frogs, hail and more, but each time Pharaoh's heart was hardened and told Moses he would not release his people."*

Then Isaiah chimed back in, *"Benjamin, please let me tell the next part."* Benjamin, though reluctantly agreed to Isaiah's request. Isaiah then shared how God told Moses that He would bring one more plague in Egypt, after that Pharaoh would let His people go.

As Isaiah was talking, I began to think to myself about this last plague and all that it involved. About midnight, God would go through Egypt and every firstborn son of Egypt would die. From the first-born son of Pharaoh who sits on the throne, to the first-born son of the slave girl and all the livestock as well. But even with all this death happening around them, God had a plan to keep His people safe and unharmed. Let me share with you the passage from the book of Exodus...

> *"Now the Lord spoke to Moses and Aaron in the land of Egypt, saying, 2 "This month shall be your beginning of months; it shall be the first month of the year to you. 3 Speak to all the congregation of Israel, saying: 'On the tenth of this month every man shall take for himself a lamb, according to the house of his father, a lamb for a household.... 5 Your lamb shall be without blemish, a male of the first year. You may take it from the sheep or from the goats. 6 Now you shall keep it until the fourteenth day of the same month. Then the whole assembly of the congregation of Israel shall kill it at twilight. 7 And they shall take some of the blood and put it on the two doorposts and on the lintel of the houses where they eat it.... 12 'For I will pass through the land of Egypt on that night, and will strike all the firstborn in*

> *the land of Egypt, both man and beast; and against all the gods of Egypt I will execute judgment: I am the Lord. 13 Now the blood shall be a sign for you on the houses where you are. And when I see the blood, I will pass over you; and the plague shall not be on you to destroy you when I strike the land of Egypt.... 24 And you shall observe this thing as an ordinance for you and your sons forever. 25 It will come to pass when you come to the land which the Lord will give you, just as He promised, that you shall keep this service. 26 And it shall be, when your children say to you, 'What do you mean by this service?' 27 that you shall say, 'It is the Passover sacrifice of the Lord, who passed over the houses of the children of Israel in Egypt when He struck the Egyptians and delivered our households.' " So the people bowed their heads and worshiped. 28 Then the children of Israel went away and did so; just as the Lord had commanded Moses and Aaron, so they did." (Exodus 12:1-3, 5-7, 12-13, 24-28 NKJV)*

At midnight, the Lord did just as He said. He struck down all the firstborn in Egypt. From the firstborn of

Pharaoh, who sat on the throne, to the firstborn of the prisoner who was in the dungeon, to the firstborn of all the livestock. All of Egypt got up during the night and there was loud wailing, for there was not a house without someone dead. As I was still thinking to myself about all of this, I heard Benjamin from across the group yell, *"Simon, are you paying attention?"* Startled, I replied, *"Yes, sorry, I was just thinking about all that you were sharing."* Benjamin then said, *"Good, you don't want to miss the best part."*

Benjamin then continued the account, *"With his heart broken from the loss of his own firstborn, Pharaoh summoned Moses and Aaron during the night and spoke. 'UP! Leave my people, you and the Israelites! Go, worship the Lord as you have requested. Take your flocks and herds as you have said and go.'"*

"Finally," Abigail said, *"God had delivered us, for the first time in 400 years God's people would know what it was like breath the air of freedom, and we were not just a free people, but we left Egypt extremely blessed. Hear what Moses wrote,"*

> *"Now the children of Israel had done according to the word of Moses, and they had asked from the Egyptians articles of*

> *silver, articles of gold, and clothing. 36 And the Lord had given the people favor in the sight of the Egyptians, so that they granted them what they requested. Thus they plundered the Egyptians." (Exodus 12:35-36 NKJV)*

Isaiah then added, *"It is like we are back paid for our 400 years of slavery in one day."*

During the rest of our journey to Jerusalem, the older men continued to tell the history of the people of Israel, of the triumphs they had when they were faithfully following God and the disasters they experienced when they lived in disobedience towards Him. I have heard these stories many times and I still like to hear them. It makes me proud of my Jewish heritage.

Chapter 3

THE ARRIVAL TO JERUSALEM

We were all so engrossed in the telling of the Jewish history that when a man shouted, *"There she is, there is Jerusalem!"* it was like we traveled through time at warp speed, being pulled from the past, right up to the present day. Looking up, I saw her in all her splendor. Even from a distance, you could see her glorious beauty. The sun was shining off the Temple, as if she was showing us the way to Jerusalem, The City of David.

As we entered the city, our entire group that

traveled together went their separate ways to their own family and friends. It was the day before the Passover and the streets were full of people buying and selling to prepare for the feast. As I made my way through the city, I came to the place where I celebrated the Passover every year. As I neared the house, my boyhood friend, Joseph Benjamin, rushed up to me in excitement, asking, *"have you seen Jesus on your way through the streets?" "Slow down, slow down, Joseph,"* I replied. *"How could I? I only have just arrived and haven't even gotten settled in. Even then, I don't even know what he looks like."* This man Jesus, I had heard stories of him and some of the amazing things he had done, but I only believed them to be stories.

Joseph then replied, *"Of course, of course, you must be tired and hungry from your journey. Come wash your feet and rest, while food is prepared. Afterwards, I will tell you everything that has happened since your last visit."*

After a long journey, any home cooked meal is good, but this one was quite exceptional. I looked at Joseph and said, *"Give my compliments to the cook". "Thank you, my friend"* Joseph replied, *"My wife is the best cook in all of Jerusalem." "Yes,"* I said with a smile,

"I can see your belt is slightly larger than the last time I saw you, she must feed you well." We both laughed and then recalled the stories of our childhood.

Upon completing our meal, Joseph said, *"Come now, have some wine, and I will tell you about Jesus and the events in Jerusalem."*

He continued, *"This man, Jesus, has become quite famous in these parts, traveling throughout all of Samaria and Judea, telling everybody about the Kingdom of heaven. He preaches repentance and the forgiveness of sins. One day He was preaching from a mountainside saying, 'Blessed are you who are poor, for yours is the kingdom of heaven. Blessed are you who hunger now, for you will be satisfied. Blessed are you who weep now, for you will laugh. Blessed are you when men hate you. When they exclude you and insult you and reject your name as evil because of the son of man.' He even said, 'We are to love our enemies.'"*

Slightly perturbed by this last comment, I blurted out, *"Love, LOVE! How in the world can we love the Romans after what they have done to us and are still doing? Tell me how?"*

Joseph, in a calm demeanor, said in return, *"Simon,*

I understand your emotion, but he has taught us, 'Do not judge and you will not be judged. Do not condemn and you will not be condemned. Forgive and you will be forgiven. Give and it will be given to you.'"

"He should preach this to the Romans," I said with bitterness growing in my voice. *"They're the ones judging everyone, not us. It's the Romans killing and torturing people."* I then took a deep breath trying to calm myself and said, *"I am sorry my friend, sometimes I let my feelings get in the way. Joseph, please continue."*

Joseph then put his hand on my shoulder. *"I understand your feeling. But Jesus is not like anyone I have seen before. He even heals people."*

"Heals?" I said in shock. *"Yes,"* he continued, *"a man blind from birth now sees, those who had leprosy have been cleansed, a paralyzed man now walks. Even a dead person has been raised back to life."*

"Now, hold it right there, Joseph." I said, *"How can a dead man be raised back to life? Only God can raise someone from the dead and perform all these miracles you have told me about."*

"Yes, I agree with you," Joseph replied, *"but there's more. He even fed five thousand men with only three fish*

and two loaves of bread. I know it sounds ridiculous, but I have friends who were there, and they are not ones to fabricate stories such as this. They had to sit in groups of fifty as his disciples came around with a basket. You could take as much as you wanted, and the basket never emptied. It was always full. Then this was the most astounding to me. My cousin Daniel was visiting up from Galilee and he heard about Jesus' disciples trying to row their boat in the middle of the night while amid a great storm. But Jesus wasn't there with them."

"Well, where was he?" I interjected.

Jospeh continued, *"I was told he was by himself on a mountain praying to his Father in Heaven, but then a disciple in the boat cried out in fear that he saw a ghost, but it was not ghost at all. IT WAS JESUS, WALKING ON THE WATER."*

Nearly spitting out my wine I blurted out, *"WALKING ON THE WHAT?!?!?!"*

"Yes, you heard me right," Joseph replied, *"walking on the water. But then Jesus called out to them and said, 'Don't fear!' And one of his chief disciples, Peter, said if it is really you, tell me to come to you. So, Jesus told him to come, and Peter walked on the water as well."*

Trying to reason with Joseph, I said, *"Well, maybe they were close to the shore or maybe your cousin was drunk and didn't get the story correct."*

Joseph replied, *"At first, I thought the same thing, but my cousin wasn't drunk, and the disciples said they were in the middle of the sea when they saw Jesus walking on the water. Who's to say that this man is not the Son of God? The deaf hear, the blind see, crippled people walking, multitudes feed on only a little food with many baskets left over. He raised the dead, calmed a storm, and walked on water."*

As Jospeh was sharing all of this, I pondered, what if what he is saying is true, what if this Jesus is the Messiah, is not God all powerful? With these thoughts rolling around in my mind, I asked him, *"What does this man Jesus say about himself?"*

With almost a look of bewilderment in his eyes of what he was about to come out of his mouth, he said with a tone of all seriousness, *"he said that the Father and I are one. Let me tell you his exact words, 'The words I say to you I do not speak on my authority. Rather, it is the Father, living in me, who is doing his work. Believe me when I say that I am in the Father and the Father is in me; or at least believe in the evidence of the works themselves.'"* *(John 14:10-12 NIV)*

I was shocked, perplexed, and almost fearful of Joseph's response as I nervously whispered, *"Is he claiming to be God? Well, what do our religious leaders say about Him?"*

"Do you remember Nicodemus?" Joseph replied, *"He is a Pharisee. I think he is beginning to believe in him, but mostly all the other leaders think Jesus is a troublemaker and want to do away with him."*

I then asked. *"Joseph, I have trusted you since childhood. What do you think of him?"*

"Well," he replied, *"from what I have seen and heard, I believe he is sent from God."* John the Baptist preached a baptism of repentance for the forgiveness of sins, and he said, *"I baptize you with water. But one more powerful than I will come, the thongs of whose sandals I am not worthy to untie. He will baptize you with the Holy Spirit and with fire." (Luke 3:16-17 NIV)* When John baptized Jesus, he came up out of the water, and a voice from heaven said; *"You are My Son, whom I love. With You I am well pleased."*

I sat back in almost a state of disbelief, not fully sure

if I just heard what I heard, but Joseph would not lie or joke with me about such things, then with my heart burning to learn more, I asked Joseph if he could take me to Jesus, so I could see him for myself. He agreed we could go the following day because Jesus had been teaching in the temple all week, but for now, it was late and time to rest.

Chapter 4

MEETING JESUS

That night, as I lay in my bed, it was difficult to rest. My mind was racing with all the things that Joseph shared with me. Did this man, Jesus, really feed 5,000 people? Did he really walk on water, did he really raise the dead? No sinful man could do the things that people are claiming he did. Is it possible that he is the promised Messiah?

When my mind finally calmed down and I began to drift off to sleep, I was suddenly aware of a noise in the background. I was so tired from being up late that at first it did not register in my mind what that sound was. I then heard it again, but, still drowsy, I dismissed it. But then I heard it a third time and knew exactly what it was. I muttered to myself, *"there's the rooster at the start of the fourth watch, and now I am awake."* Everyone else in the house seemed to be sound asleep, but I was not. *"Well, so much for my good night's rest. I might as well get up and go for a walk through the city. Maybe that will calm my mind."*

I walked outside and saw many memories all around me. There was the same water pot that Joseph's neighbor had been using since we were kids. Then, as I walked down the street, I laughed to myself when I saw the same uneven, raised stone that was still not fixed on the walking path. I remember tripping over that thing every time that we ran as we were playing.

This walk I was on was seeming to do the trick. I was feeling calmer and was about to head back to the house, when I suddenly I heard yelling voices that made my heart rush. Maybe this walk wasn't such a good idea, so I backed into a doorway, thinking it may be thieves looking for prey. As I waited. I saw it was Roman soldiers, and they were escorting a prisoner through the streets. I wondered who the man was that they were leading, what had he done, and what would be his end. As they came closer to where I was, I could see that he was bloody and bruised. *"He must have been in a fight with somebody, and he got caught"*, I said to myself.

As they were passing by, I tried to hide even more in that tiny doorway, trying not to get in the way or get involved, but as they passed, the man they were leading looked over at me and when our eyes met, a shock shot through my very being, it wasn't so much a feeling of fear, but one of amazement. He did not have the eyes of a criminal. Who was this man? It was like everything and everyone disappeared around me and an amazement at what I was seeing consumed me.

Then I was jolted back to the reality of what was happening when I heard the Roman soldier shouting, *"move it Jew dog,"* at the man they were leading.

What could He possibly have done to be led away like this? So, I began to follow from a distance. As I followed, I saw they were leading him to where Pontius Pilate, the governor of Judaea, made his rulings. As I saw them lead him in, I stopped and thought to myself, *"should I go get Joseph? But if I do that, I might miss what is going on here."* After a few moments of debating with myself, I decided to go into the courtyard to find out more. But by the time I had gotten in there. I could already hear many voices shouting, *"Away with him! Give us Barabbas."* Not knowing who Barabbas was, I asked the man next to me and he explained that Barabbas was a rebel and a murderer. I then asked who the man next to him was, the one with the purple robe and the crown of thorns because I had just seen the Roman soldiers leading him through the streets.

Suddenly, we were interrupted when Pilate raised his hand and said, *"I am bringing this man out to you to let you know I find no charge against him. And you are asking me to release Barabbas, a murderer? What do you want me to do with this other man, Jesus?"*

"Wait, what?" I thought to myself, *"that is Jesus, the man Joseph was telling me about? How can this be? What did he do?"* Then, to my horror, the crowd chanted, *"Crucify him! Crucify him!"*

My heart sank in disbelief, and you could see the same look on Pilate's face as he proclaimed to the crowed, *"What? Crucify him? For what, I find no basis for a charge against him. If you want to crucify him, then you do it?"*

I turned to the man I had been talking to just a moment before, and with my emotions beginning to run wild in my eyes, I looked at him and said, *"What did He do? What crime did He commit? This crowd is calling for His death?"* With an annoyed look on his face that I was bothering him again, he said, *"I am not fully sure, but I believe the religious leaders want to kill him because he claims to be the Son of God."* In shock I gasped, *"What! The Son of God?"* Then the man with more of a serious tone in his voice pointed at my chest and said, *"Are you one of His followers?"* In fear, I immediately spouted back, *"No, I am not." "OK, well then, keep quiet,"* he jolted, *"I am only doing what the religious leaders are telling us to do. If you want to know more, go ask one of the Pharisees who is in charge. Now leave me alone."*

My attention immediately turned back to Pilate when I heard him say, *"I am innocent of this man's blood. It is your responsibility!"* Then the crowd yelled back in response, *"Let His blood be on us and our children!"*

Their response startled me to the very core of my being. I thought to myself, *"what have they done?"* Then out of nowhere these words came out of my mouth, *"They can't do this to him."* At that moment, there were several people around me that were convinced that I was one of Jesus' followers and was trying to defend him. They pushed me out of the courtyard and then out of fear of what might happen to me, I loosed myself from their grip and ran away from them as fast as possible. In panic, I prayed, *"God help me, I need to find Joseph. Please help me."*

I turned down several streets, trying to find my way through the city, but with all that was happening I was confused and very turned around, I just couldn't seem to find where I was going. I then stopped and breathed, trying to regain my composer, after a moment, I looked up and saw that I was only a few streets away from Joseph's house. I took just one more moment before venturing out and then tried to cross from the street I was on to the next, but my timing could not have been worse. When I turned the corner, I met the soldiers and the crowd right in front of me. I tried to back up and hide, but it was too late. The Roman looked at me and said, *"STOP, get over there and help him carry that cross!"* I looked at the soldier in complete fear and my mind raced, thinking about trying to run for my life, but then I saw him put his hand on his sword and my life flashed before my eyes, because when a Roman soldier draws his sword, it is not normally put away unless there is blood on it. One of the other soldiers then grabbed me by the arm and began to lead me to the cross. When we got to the cross, I looked down and there was Jesus, lying on the ground with a heavy beam on top of him. I then tried to pull away from the soldier, but he tightened his grip on my arm, and again pointed at Jesus lying on the ground. He then threw me towards the cross and told me to carry it. Looking at the soldier with his hand on his sword and then at Jesus lying in the middle of the road, I thought it best to help carry the cross. As I bent down to help Jesus, my thoughts were running wild within me. *"This cannot be happening. Of all the surrounding people, the Roman had to pick me."* My mind then turned to the crowd, would they all think I was a criminal as well? Being overwhelmed by everything happening, I shouted to the crowd, *"I am innocent of any crime this man did, and I am not responsible for his blood."*

As I took the weight of the cross on my shoulder, blood ran down my hand, but it was not my blood. It was his, and he was still lying on the ground. Trembling, I looked at the soldier and said, *"I think your prisoner is dead."* He sharply responded to me, *"He is not dead, he is still breathing, now get moving before I lose my patience and nail you to his cross."* I could not believe that he was still alive, with his body all cut up the way it was. I told him to just lie there and die, but to my amazement, he reached up and grabbed my leg, pulling himself up and putting his hands around the cross next to mine. Then something miraculous happened that to this day I cannot fully explain. When his hand touched mine, even in the middle of all the chaos, I felt something go through me, a peace that I had never experienced before. I felt a sense of love for the man, because I could feel his love radiating towards me. Then he looked at me and the look in his eyes made everything around us seemingly disappear for a moment and instantly my heart changed from trying to get out of this situation, to a friend helping a friend in need.

I then became fully aware of all the people around us and what they were saying to him. Some were cursing and spitting at him and others were crying and mourning for him.

Just then, as we were trying to walk, our feet got tangled, and we fell to the ground hard. He let out an agonizing groan of pain and I truly thought he was about to die. Then in anger, the Roman soldier, because we were not moving as fast as he would have liked, raised his whip over his head and was about to lash us, but I yelled, *"Haven't you done enough to him already? Can't you tell he is about dead?"* I lifted the cross from his body, thinking that he was dead, but then he rolled over and began to stand back up. At that moment, I just happened to look over and saw a slight look of disbelief beginning to form in the eyes of the soldier. He quietly muttered to himself, *"How can this be? After everything he has been through, he's still alive, but has not given up?"*

Then from the crowd, a woman came over and gave me and Jesus a drink of water. Then Jesus looked at the women there with her, and said to them, *"Daughters of Jerusalem, do not weep for me; weep for yourselves and for your children. For the time will come when you say, 'Blessed are the barren women, the wombs that never bore and the breasts that never nursed! Then they will say to the mountains, "fall on us!" and to the hill, "cover us!" For if men do these things when the tree is green, what will happen when it is dry?" (Luke 23:28-31 NKJV)*

As he was saying this, I looked at the soldiers, they were standing still, not moving at all. I looked back down at Jesus in amazement. He was being led to his death and was telling these women not to weep for him. But then, we were all jolted back to the task at hand when another Roman soldier came up behind us and pushed us along and telling us to get moving.

I reached out my hand towards Jesus to help him the rest of the way to his feet. As he stood up, we both got under the cross to carry it together. He looked at me with a smile on his face and then looked up the hill, knowing it was his destination. From that moment on, any feelings of why those soldiers picked me vanished and a new heart was being birthed towards this man they called Jesus. I felt that even in this man's innocence, there was something larger going on.

Chapter 5

THE CLIMB TO THE END

As we got closer to the top of the hill where Jesus was to be crucified, tears filled my eyes and I had a lump in my throat from hearing the cries of the others already being nailed to their crosses. It's a sound I will never forget. The sound of the hammer hitting the nail and the men screaming at the top of their lungs, all the while trying to fight against the soldiers for their lives. I looked and Jesus was still walking beside me, embracing the cross.

When we finally arrived, one of the soldiers who had been waiting for us at the top of that hill shoved us from behind and we both fell to the ground. At the sight of us falling, another group of soldiers began laughing. I pushed the cross off both of us and then tried to help Jesus up off the ground. Right before I could, another soldier came up to me with a spear in his hand, yelling, *"Back away from the prisoner, or I will kill you where you stand."* I looked at Jesus and just one glance into his eyes communicated a thousand words. It was like he was saying, *"it's ok, I must do what I am about to do, do not worry."*

I did not fully understand; I wanted to feel the anger towards the soldiers, but I also wanted to do what Jesus wanted me to do, so I turned and walked over to a group of people who looked like they were his followers and I looked at them with tears in my eyes shaking my head, wondering why...why are they treating him this way? A woman then walked up to me and put her age-old hands on my face, holding it as if she was holding a child who was scared. I could see love in her eyes, a love that only a mother could give to a child. She told me, *"Do not to fear, for therefore he was born." "Born for this?"* I responded, *"no one in their right mind wants to be crucified, no one."* She pulled me closer to her face and said, *"I am Jesus' mother. One night, an angel of the Lord came to me and told me I was going to conceive a child, while never knowing a man, and I was to give him the name Jesus because he will save his people from their sins."*

"Save us from our sins?" I retorted, *"By being crucified, murdered by a group of madmen. How can he save us if he's dead?"* I pulled her hands away from my face and then looked over to where Jesus was.

The soldiers were gathering around him. It was now his turn to be crucified. As I was watching, Jesus' mother wrapped her hands around my arm. She looked up at me with fear in her eyes as we watched what was about to happen.

The soldiers rolled the cross over to its proper position. When they turned back around to carry Jesus over, he was already crawling towards the cross as if he was ready to be crucified. The soldiers looked at each other in disbelief, wondering what was happening. It looked as if they did not know what to do until the Centurion yelled at them, *"Get moving!"*

Then one of them grabbed Jesus by the hand, pulled him up onto the cross, and held him in place. The other soldier pulled his arm to the beam and gripped it against the cross. As this was going on, I could hear another group of people yelling at the soldiers to hurry and get him on the cross. I turned to those around me and asked, *"Don't these people know he is innocent?"* Then a man came over and put his hand on my shoulder and said, *"That is the sad thing, they know he is innocent"* I answered angrily, *"Then why are they treating him this way?"* His response made me even more angry, *"It is because our religious leaders wanted him out of the way, for he was challenging their authority."* I could not believe what I was hearing. *"They are putting him to death because of jealousy. That's no cause for the death".* But then my heart softened when I looked down at Jesus' mother, who was still holding on to my arm. I could see her eyes get bigger and feel her grip tighten as the soldier raised the hammer over his head and brought it down to the nail. Right before the sound of the hammer hitting the nail rang out on the top of that hill, I felt her hide her eyes as she turned her face into my chest and jumped as if she was the one in pain. She cried, *"No, no, no!"* I put my other arm around her to help comfort her. We then heard three more hits of the hammer on the first nail.

As they stretched out his other arm, we heard one soldier comment, *"this one is no fun. He is not even fighting us. It is almost as if he wants to die. Let's just get this over with."*

One of Jesus' supporters, who was standing next to me, began to quote the prophet Isaiah from the scriptures and as he spoke, it was like he was finally understanding these prophecies were coming to pass right before his very eyes. He said, *"He was oppressed, and He was afflicted, Yet He opened not His mouth; He was led as a lamb to the slaughter, and as a sheep before its shearers is silent, So He opened not His mouth."* (Isaiah 53:7 NKJV)

And then the man beside him with the same realization of what was happening quoted from the Psalms, *"For dogs have surrounded Me; The congregation of the wicked has enclosed me. They pierced My hands and My feet;"* (Psalm 22:16 NKJV)

I asked the first man who he was, and he responded, *"My name is Nicodemus, and I am one of his followers. What is your name?"* After I told him my name, I explained all that had happened since I arrived in Jerusalem, and how the soldiers had made me help carry the cross. Then with tears in my eyes I explained to Nicodemus the man I was before meeting Jesus, how I was more concerned about myself and what others thought of me rather than the pain that Jesus was in, but then Nicodemus interrupted me saying, *"but then something happened, didn't it? I was following the crowd the whole time and saw the change in your face and in your heart when Jesus looked into your eyes."* With tears still pouring down my face, I said, *"His eyes carry a love I have never experienced before."*

Then a man standing beside us whispered with intensity, *"Nicodemus, Nicodemus, do you see that?"* We both turned to see what was happening and Nicodemus said, *"truly he must be who he said he was, the Son of the living God because the scriptures continue to confirm him"* Then Nicodemus said to me, *"have you ever read in the book of Psalms where it says 'They divide my clothing among them and cast lots for my garment.'" I replied, "Yes, I believe I remember that"* and he pointed at the Roman soldiers who were sitting to the side of the cross gambling for the garments of Jesus.

As I looked over at the soldiers, I glimpsed at Jesus' mutilated body and this time something was different, I went from thinking Jesus is like no one I have ever met, to feeling a deep sense of guilt, horror, and shame, and then these thoughts bombarded my mind, *"That innocent man on the cross, who was flogged, ridiculed, and beaten, you were the one who helped carry the cross, you helped the Romans kill him"* I looked at Nicodemus and it was like God had given him a doorway into my mind as he said, *"Simon, let your heart be at peace, let me tell you what Jesus shared with us just a few days ago. He said, 'We are going up to Jerusalem, and everything that is written by the prophets about the Son of Man will be fulfilled. He will be handed over to the gentiles. They will mock him, insult him, spit on him, flog him and kill him.' Simon, you are not destroying God's plan, you were just part of fulfilling it".*

Just then Jesus' mother pulled on my arm and said, *"listen he's about to say something."* We all turned our hearts and ears towards Jesus, and we heard him say in a strained voice, *"Father, forgive them for they know not what they are doing!"*

One soldier looked up at Jesus and said to him; *"It's a little too late to ask for forgiveness."* The soldier then looked at us and said, *"May this be a lesson to you, that you should ask for forgiveness before sentencing. See the pain your friend is in?"*

I turned back to Nicodemus and said, *"can you explain this to me, how he can ask God to forgive these people who are doing so much wrong to him?"* We were then interrupted by the surrounding people who were looking at the sky, wondering why it had gotten so dark. One man even asked, *"Is it that late in the day?"* Nicodemus replied, *"No, it is only the sixth hour."* Then all our attention was turned back to Jesus as He cried out in a loud voice, *"Eloi, Eloi, lama sabachthani?"*

Some in the crowd said, *"He's calling Elijah."* Then someone ran and got a sponge filled with wine vinegar, put it on a stick and offered it to Jesus to drink. Someone in the crowd said, *"No, leave him alone. Let's see if Elijah comes to save him."*

Then Jesus, from the cross, looked over to where we were and spoke to his mother, who was still holding onto my arm, and to another man standing beside her, *"Dear mother, here is your son,"* he looked at a man standing next to her and said, *"Here is your mother."*

Nicodemus explained to me that the man's name was John and how he was one of the twelve disciples that Jesus called to follow him. Jesus then called out with a loud voice, saying, *"Father, into your hands I commit my spirit."* He then bowed his head and breathed his last breath.

For just a moment, it seemed like the whole earth went silent. Even the centurion took off his helmet. He looked at the sky and how black it was, and then looked over at Jesus. He took a couple of steps back and then just looked at us and then looked back at Jesus; it was almost like he saw everything that was happening, and he knew down to his very core that something else was about to take place. The other soldiers were watching the centurion, waiting for a command of what to do. Then the earth shook, and the rocks split. Some people ran for their lives while others laid on the ground waiting for the quaking to stop. Then everything suddenly went silent again, and the centurion, with a pale face, looked back at Jesus and said, *"Surely, he was the Son of God!"*

Then the two criminals began screaming and crying out for help to the soldiers, as they were pulling on the nails, trying to set themselves free, but the soldiers were in a state of shock at what was happening. They were just standing there looking at Jesus.

Then all our attention turned to a man running up the hill. He ran towards the religious leaders yelling to them that the curtain in the temple had torn in two from the top to the bottom during the earthquake.

I looked over at Nicodemus like I didn't know what to fully believe. Could all this really be happening? Could Jesus really be dead? Then another man came up the hill and handed the centurion a piece of paper. I asked Nicodemus, *"who is he?"* He replied, *"that is Joseph of Arimathea. He's one of Jerusalem's leaders."* With my heart sinking even lower I said, *"what could he possibly want with Jesus? He can't accuse him of more wrongdoing. He is already dead."* Nicodemus, with compassion in his heart, said to me, *"Oh, Simon, do not worry, he is a follower of Jesus also, just like I am."*

After the soldier finished reading the paper, Jospeh walked over to Nicodemus and informed him that Pilate had given written permission for him to take the body for burial after Jesus had died. Then the centurion looked up at Jesus and ordered one soldier to pierce his side to make sure he was dead. When he did, blood and water came out. Then he ordered another soldier to take a mallet and break the legs of the two criminals. They let out a scream that I will not forget for a long time and then, because they could not push themselves up to get a breath of air, they slowly died of suffocation.

When the two criminals were dead, the centurion ordered his soldiers to take Jesus off his cross and turn him over to Joseph. But then he did something that you never see a centurion do. He told his soldiers to lower Jesus and handle his body with respect. When they turned his body over to us, I glanced at the centurion, who had tears in his eyes. He then noticed me looking at him and quickly turned and walked away.

Chapter 6

THE BURIAL

As we walked down the hill where Jesus was crucified, we felt hopeless, confused, and destitute. While carrying his body, Joseph told us he had just carved out a tomb for his burial and that it was close by. We took him and laid him in the new tomb, rolled an enormous stone in front of the entrance and then went our separate ways because the next day was the Sabbath, and it was a commandment not to do any work on that day.

Right before we all went left, I walked up to John and asked if I could come and talk with him after the Sabbath. I had so many questions that I felt I needed answered. He agreed and then I left to go back to my friend Joseph Benjamin's house.

I was walking down the street in a state of bewilderment. I could sense people all around me, but it was like I was all alone. But then I looked down the street at the people who were coming towards me and as our eyes met, they all had a look of astonishment, and they moved to the opposite side of the road as if to get away from me. I then turned around and people were keeping their distance, pointing and talking about me. At first, I did not know what was going on. I then looked down at my clothes and realized that I was covered in blood. His blood, Jesus' blood.

I turned and walked towards the people. I felt frustration rise within me. *"What are you looking at?"* I yelled, *"See this blood? You put this blood on me. This is the blood of the man you had crucified today; this is the blood of the man the Romans flogged today; this is the blood from the cross he carried until I was forced to carry it for him by the soldiers to the place where he was crucified. This is innocent blood you put on me when you helped condemn an innocent man."* I was yelling like a wild man in the middle of the street, showing them the bloodstains on my shirt and hands. I then wept profusely and turned and walked away because I knew they only did what they did because they listened to the religious leaders.

As I came to the house, Joseph was outside. He said with a gasp, *"Simon, what happened to you? Are you alright? Do you need a doctor?"* I looked at him with my eyes still full of tears and said, *"I am ok, this is not my blood, and I am not in trouble, I will explain all that happened to me but first I need a few moments to get cleaned up."* Joseph opened the door and let me inside.

That evening, after I had washed all the blood off my body and put on new clothes, I just sat in my room alone in silence and wept, trying to process all the emotions I had gone through.

I then heard a quiet knock on the door, and Jospeh said, *"If you are ready, dinner has been prepared."*

As we sat together and ate, I shared all that had happened, my sleepless night, wondering down the street and seeing Jesus for the first time, experiencing the fear of hearing the crowd condemn him to die, the Roman soldiers making me help carry the cross, the sound of the nails being beaten into his body, the followers of Jesus I had met, the horror of the screams from the criminals dying, and the shaking of the earth as Jesus died. As I shared these things, I could see tears beginning to flow down the face of Joseph and of his wife Ruth, for they had both heard and believed the Jesus was from God. After sharing all that had happened that day, it was very late, and we agreed we should try to get some rest and talk about this more in the morning.

Chapter 7

THE WAITING

The next day, the three of us talked all day. I shared with them some scriptures that I had heard from Jesus' followers while he was being crucified. Joseph and Ruth understood exactly what I was talking about, but no hope filled our hearts because our hope seemed to die with Jesus.

With all my heart I wanted to go see Nicodemus and John, but it was the Sabbath and, according to the Law, we could not leave our homes until after it was over.

The next morning, I woke up when my bed started

shaking again, and just as suddenly as it started, the shaking stopped. I ran out of my room and asked if everyone was OK. When I was assured that we were safe, we all sat down to breakfast. After we ate, and with anticipation in my heart, me and Jospeh left the house to go find John.

As we walked down the street, I was watching the people around us, and they were talking with each other about the normality of life. It was just like another day to them, like Jesus had never died. We arrived at the place where John was staying and when I got to the door, I could hear them inside talking, with my heart racing, I took a deep breath and then knocked, when I did, the muffled voices I heard inside became quiet. Again, I knocked, and then a voice quietly responded, *"who is it?"* I breathed out and said, *"my name is Simon of Cyrene. I am the man who the Romans forced to carry Jesus' cross. If you don't believe me, ask John. He saw me there when Jesus was crucified and told me he was staying here."* The door slowly opened, and it was John standing there. He looked at me and smiled and then said, *"Simon, come in quickly. We thought you might have been the soldiers coming to arrest us."* I looked at him puzzled and said, *"We just walked through the streets and saw no soldiers, and why would they want to arrest you?"* John leaned in closer and whispered, *"The body of Jesus is gone." "Gone?"* I gasped, *"Why would anybody want to steal the body of Jesus, after what they did to him?" "I don't know,"* John replied, *"but when the women in our group went down to the tomb early this morning to anoint his body with oil, they got there and saw that the tomb was open. Someone had rolled the stone away from the tomb entrance."*

Someone from the other side of the room said, *"let Mary tell them what happened. She can tell the story better than you."*

I looked at Mary; but her face looked different from the others in the room, there was hope and joy in her eyes, and she began, *"I have shared with them but they do not believe me. As I was walking to the tomb with Mary, the mother of James, we wondered who was going to help us roll the stone back away from the entrance of the tomb? Right before we got there, another earthquake hit, just like we felt the day he died. After the earthquake stopped, we hurried to the tomb, finding that the stone had already been rolled away, and we were astonished to see an angel of the Lord sitting on top of the stone. The angel then spoke to us. The angel said, 'Do not be afraid, for I know you are looking for Jesus, who was crucified.*

He is not here; He is risen, just as He said. Come and see the place where He lay.' So, we went in to see his body, but it was not there, it was gone, only his linen was there where he once laid. Then the angel instructed us to hurry and inform his disciples: 'He has risen from the dead and is going before you to Galilee. There, you will see him.'"

"So, we ran back to the house and told them what had happened. Before I could finish, Peter looked at me and then ran out the door, and John quickly followed him. They came back some time later. I asked them what they saw. He said that the guards were gone and that the tomb was empty. He entered the tomb, saw the cloth folded up, separate from the linen and yet he still does not believe."

Peter responded in haste, *"I believe you, Mary, what you saw. I just don't understand."*

Just then, I heard another voice from across the room. *"None of you are making any sense. Just accept that he is gone. I am leaving and I hope you all will as well."*

There was silence in the room for some time and no one knew quite what to say. So, I leaned over to Joseph and asked if we should give them some time to themselves. He agreed, and he also reminded me that the group I had traveled with to Jerusalem was leaving in the morning. I felt my heart begin to sink because I began to realize that I might not see some people again and all the question that I had would go unanswered. As we turned to leave, Mary, the mother of Jesus, grabbed me by the arm, she looked me in the eye and said, *"I know it was not your choice to help carry that cross, but as a mother I want to say thank you for helping him when he needed it."* With tears in her eyes, we embraced and then me and Joseph took our leave.

As we left, we walked down the street in silence. As we turned the corner two men were running towards us. Joseph grabbed me by the edge of my coat and pulled me out of the way just in time. I looked at Joseph in astonishment, wondering where in the world they could go in such a hurry.

Chapter 8

MY LIFE IS CHANGED FOREVER

The next morning, I arose early and told Joseph that I wanted to try to stop by and try to see Peter, James, and John before I joined the others I traveled with back to Cyrene.

I walked back to the house where we were all the day before, I knocked on the door and said, *"John, it is Simon, I just wanted to say good..."* Before I could finish the word goodbye, Peter swung open the door and said, *"He's alive, He's alive, Simon."* Startled, I looked back at him and said, *"Who's alive, Peter?"* He exclaimed,

"Jesus, He's alive! He's alive! Right after you left, our friend Cleopas came to us saying that he and a friend were walking to Emmaus when a man came up to them and asked what they were talking about. They shared with 'this stranger' all that had happened in Jerusalem and how Jesus had been crucified." Peter then stopped and said, *"Wait, I want Cleopas to finished this story."* As Cleopas walked over to us, I said in bewilderment, *"Wait, aren't you one of the men that almost ran us over yesterday as you were running through the street?"* Cleopas replied, *"Was that you? I am so sorry, but we were in such a hurry we probably ran into many people, because as Peter was saying, after we arrived at our destination with 'the stranger' we were traveling with, we invited Him in to stay with us. As we sat down to eat, He took some bread, blessed it, and then broke it. As soon as He did that, we realized who this stranger was– IT WAS JESUS!"*

Peter then shared that after he had heard this from Cleopas, all the doors remained shut and locked, and then Jesus suddenly appeared in the middle of them all, right in this very room. I looked at Peter in disbelief and said, *"Peter, are you sure" "Yes,"* he exclaimed, *"He even ate food right in front of us, He then showed us the nail prints in His hands and feet and told us to touch Him so all doubt would leave us. He was not a ghost."*

"Simon," Peter continued, *"I now understand Jesus' purpose. It was not to save us from the Romans, it was to save us from our sin. John the Baptist was right. Jesus really is the Lamb of God who, through His death, burial, and resurrection, takes away the sins of the world."*

I stood astonished by all that I was hearing that this man, Jesus, was much more than just a good man. He was much more than just a wonderful teacher; He was much more than just a prophet sent from God. He was the very Son of God who came and lived a perfect, sinless life, experiencing all the pain, suffering, and temptations that we faced, yet He did not sin. He truly is as the John the Baptist said of Him. He is The Lamb of God who takes away the sin of the world!

Because of Jesus' sacrifice, all can be restored back to God in a relationship if they accept what Jesus did on that cross.

As I started this journey with you, I said this was a Passover week I could never forget. It started out as a remembrance of the deliverance that God gave His people from slavery to the Egyptians. Then, it turned into the beginning of a deliverance for all mankind from the power of sin. With Passover, it all began with the blood of a lamb spread across the doorposts. With salvation for all men, it began with the blood of ONE MAN poured out on a cross.

Chapter 9

RESTORATION

But how, how does this work? How can we be restored back to God through Jesus?

The answer to this is very simple. It is as simple as ABC.

First, we must Admit. We must admit that by our very nature we are sinners. Sin entered this world when Adam the first man, listened to what the devil said, instead of obeying what God has spoken to him.

> *Therefore, just as through one man sin entered the world, and death through sin,*

and thus death spread to all men, because all sinned. Romans 5:12 NKJV

We must also admit that there is nothing we can do to fix ourselves, we need a Savior to free us from our sin.

Second, we must Believe. We must believe that Jesus died on the cross for the payment of our sins and then tree days later, God raised Him from the dead.

Therefore, as through one man's offense judgment came to all men, resulting in condemnation, even so through one Man's righteous act the free gift came to all men, resulting in justification of life. 19 For as by one man's disobedience many were made sinners, so also by one Man's obedience many will be made righteous. Romans 5:18-19 NKJV

And He Himself is the propitiation for our sins, and not for ours only but also for the whole world.1 John 2:2 NKJV

Third, we must Confess. We must confess that Jesus Christ is the Lord and Savior of our life. Accepting what Jesus did on the cross is so much more than just a one way ticket to Heaven when we die, it is a complete restoration to what God intended for man to be. Our model and example is Jesus Christ. That is why He must be Lord of our life. We look to Him and the life He lived to give us direction and guidance.

> *that if you confess with your mouth the Lord Jesus and believe in your heart that God has raised Him from the dead, you will be saved. 10 For with the heart one believes unto righteousness, and with the mouth confession is made unto salvation. Romans 10:9-10 NKJV*

If you know you need Jesus because of the sin problem in your life, you can pray this prayer now.

"Lord Jesus, I know and admit openly I am a sinner. I do believe You died for my sins and rose from the dead. I choose today to turn from my sins and invite You to come into my heart and life. I now, by the grace of God choose to trust and follow Your leading in my life as I confess You as my Lord and Savior. In Jesus' Name. Amen".

If you prayed this prayer of salvation and committment to Jesus, I now encourage you to find a

Bible believing church to begin attending and learning more about what God says in His Word, the Bible.

Made in the USA
Monee, IL
06 April 2025

15132920R00039